Daniel Goes to the Dentist

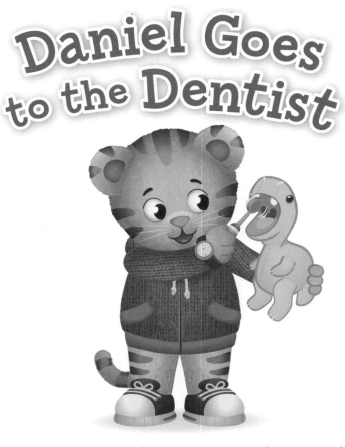

Adapted by Alexandra Cassel Schwartz
Based on the screenplay "Daniel Visits the Dentist" written by Kevin Monk
Poses and layouts by Jason Fruchter

Simon Spotlight
New York   London   Toronto   Sydney   New Delhi

SIMON SPOTLIGHT
An imprint of Simon & Schuster Children's Publishing Division
1230 Avenue of the Americas, New York, New York 10020
This Simon Spotlight paperback edition August 2019
© 2019 The Fred Rogers Company
SIMON SPOTLIGHT and colophon are registered trademarks of Simon & Schuster, Inc.
For information about special discounts for bulk purchases, please contact Simon & Schuster
Special Sales at 1-866-506-1949 or business@simonandschuster.com.
Manufactured in the United States of America 0621 LAK
10 9 8 7 6
ISBN 978-1-5344-4909-1
ISBN 978-1-5344-4910-7 (eBook)

"Great job today, Daniel," Dr. Plat said. "You stayed still and kept your mouth open wide for me. Make sure to keep brushing!"

Dr. Plat gave Daniel a special dentist sticker and a new toothbrush, too!

"Thank you!" said Daniel.

"I liked going to the dentist today," said Daniel. "When you do something new, it can help to talk about what you'll do. Ugga Mugga!"

At the end of his checkup, Daniel felt his teeth with his tongue. "Wow! They feel so nice and smooth!" he said.

After she finished cleaning, Dr. Plat sprayed some cool water into Daniel's mouth. Then she slurped all the water away.

Daniel opened his mouth and did a quiet roar. *Bzzzz!* The polisher swirled around Daniel's mouth. He tried to talk, but he couldn't get his words out!

"What did you say?" Dr. Plat asked. "I know it's hard to talk while I'm brushing."

"I said, 'it feels different!'" Daniel said.

Then Dr. Plat asked Daniel which toothpaste flavor he wanted: vanilla or berry-striped mint.

"Grr-ific!" Daniel said. "I choose berry-striped mint!"

Bzzzz! The tooth polisher made a loud noise.
"Will it hurt?" Daniel asked, worried. Dr. Plat let him feel
the polisher on his paw. *Bzzzz!* "It doesn't hurt. It tickles!"
Daniel giggled.

BZZZZ!

Now it was time for Dr. Plat to look at Daniel's teeth, but when Daniel saw all of the dentist's tools, he felt a little nervous again.

♪ *"When we do something new, let's talk about what we'll do,"* Dr. Plat sang. She showed Daniel the little mirror she uses to see inside his mouth. She also had a special tooth polisher that takes off all the bad germs—even the ones that are really hard to reach!

Then Dr. Plat put gloves on her hands and a mask on her face.
Dr. Plat looked a little different, but it was still her!

Dr. Plat clipped on a bib over Daniel's sweater.

"A bib?" Daniel said, confused. "My baby sister, Margaret, wears a bib."

Dr. Plat explained that everyone wears a bib at the dentist . . . even grown-ups! The bib would help keep Daniel's sweater clean and dry during his checkup.

Imagining made the wait go by quickly. Soon Dr. Plat led Daniel and Mom into her office. It had a big lamp and a comfy chair that leaned back.

Show me your quiet roar and open up wide, brush up and down and brush side to side!

Brush morning and night, you know what I mean, brushing helps keep our teeth healthy and clean!"

Daniel sang,
"I'm going to brush
those teeth until
they're clean
and bright.

Brush, brush, brush
until they're shiny
and white!

Daniel pretended to brush Mr. Dino's teeth. "I wonder what it would be like to be a dentist," Daniel said. He imagined that he was a dentist for many different animals!

When Daniel and Mom arrived at the dentist's office, they waited in the waiting room. It had many toys, like Mr. Dino and a pretend dentist kit!

During the checkup, Daniel would need to sit still and open his mouth wide, as if he was doing a quiet roar. "Roar!" Daniel whispered.

Now it was time to go to the dentist, but Daniel was feeling one-stripe nervous.

🎵 *"When we do something new, let's talk about what we'll do,"* 🎵 Mom Tiger sang. She explained that the dentist, Dr. Plat, would look inside Daniel's mouth to make sure his teeth are healthy.

Mom Tiger put toothpaste on Daniel's toothbrush. Then she sang,
"First you brush the top teeth,
brush the top and don't stop.
Then you brush the bottom teeth,
brush the bottom and make sure that you've got them!
Brush every morning and night,
brush off those germs and make your teeth all right!"

Daniel likes brushing his teeth in the morning and at bedtime, too. It makes his teeth feel smooth and clean.

"Like this?" asked Daniel. He pretended to brush Tigey's teeth.

"Just like that!" replied Mom Tiger. "Now before we go, let's brush *your* teeth."

It was a beautiful day in the neighborhood. Daniel was going to visit his new dentist, Dr. Plat.

"A dentist is a doctor for your teeth," Mom Tiger explained. "Today we're going for a checkup so Dr. Plat can make sure your teeth are clean."